Where Are You?

For Kate Burns - with thanks
F.S.

For my mother and in memory
of my father
D.M.

British Library Cataloguing in Publication Data
A catalogue record of this book is available from the British Library

HB ISBN 0 340 71456 5
PB ISBN 0 340 71457 3

Text copyright © Francesca Simon 1998
Illustration © David Melling 1998

The right of Francesca Simon to be identified as the author of the text of this work
and of David Melling to be identified as the illustrator of this work has been
asserted by them in accordance with the Copyright, Design and Patents Act 1988.

First hb edition published 1998
First pb edition published 1998

10 9 8 7 6 5 4 3 2 1

Published by Hodder Children's Books,
a division of Hodder Headline plc,
338 Euston Road, London NW1 3BH

Printed in Belgium

Where Are You?

Francesca Simon • David Melling

Hodder
Children's
Books

A division of Hodder Headline plc

One day Harry and Grandpa
went to the supermarket.
Harry had never been in such
a wonderful place before.

Suddenly Harry sniffed the most delicious smell.

"Yum . . . cake!" said Harry.

ZIP!

Off he went.

"We need apples," said Grandpa.
"We need pizza.
We need . . ."

"Harry? Harry? Where are you?"

"He's not under the bananas."

"He's not under the lettuce."

" He's *not* under the beans."

Then suddenly...

"Ah, there you are, Harry!" said Grandpa.

SNATCH!

"Pardon me," said Grandpa. "Have you seen Harry?"

"He went that-a-way," said Mrs Ruffle.
"Harry! Where are you?" said Grandpa.

Harry was on the cake trail.

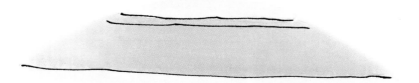

"Cold," said Harry, "**BRRRR**".

"Slippy," said Harry.

"*WHEEEE*."

The cakes were getting closer.

"Harry! Where are you?" said Grandpa.

Then Harry saw the cakes.

"We need cake, Grandpa,"
said Harry.

"Grandpa?"

Harry stood still.

"You're not Grandpa.
You're not Grandpa."
Then suddenly . . .

"There you are, Grandpa!" said Harry.

"You're not Grandpa!
GRANDPA! WHERE ARE YOU?"

"HARRY! WHERE ARE YOU?"

BUMP!

"You were lost, Grandpa," said Harry.
"You were lost, Harry," said Grandpa.

"But now we're found."

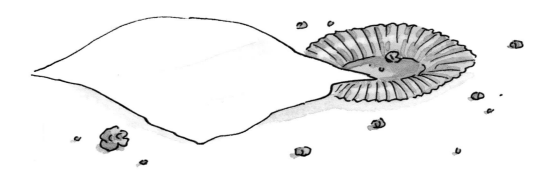